AROUND ME

P Y EMMANUEL JOY

Made with ♥ on the Notion Press Platform
www.notionpress.com

This Book is Dedicated to all the people who inspired to write this book.

Contents

Foreword *vii*

1. Nature For Future... 1
2. Where There Is A Will There Is A Way.. 6
3. Transformation Begins With Teacher 9
4. Money Matters.... 13
5. Humanity Matters 18
6. The True Valentine 22
7. Before It's Too Late.... 26

Foreword

Around Me!!!

This is my second book, There is so much that we can learn from our surroundings, here I have written the incidents, experiences which made me to learn something , some are in stories and some are my experiences , I believe that this book will also be helpful for the readers to understand the life better, each and everyday life teaches us so many things that will enrich us to suceed in life either through our life or through others, some experiences can help to us correct ourselves , so lets learn from our surrounding and lead a happy life, I hope this book gives you some message and helps you to develop more....

Happy Reading !!!

P Y Emmanuel Joy

CHAPTER ONE

NATURE FOR FUTURE...

Nature a wonderful gift from God to mankind, life on earth is possible only because of this wonderful nature, God gave this nature i.e land, water and air for free of cost, but today due to the Greediness of Humans we are not only paying for everything but also destroying this nature.....Though nature is warning us through so many ways like floods, land slides etc but we are not taking that as serious if this continues there will be no life existing on earth in future, it is our responsibility to save the nature for our better future....As Gandhi said Earth has enough for man's need and not greed...

There lived a man named Joy, he was born and bought up in a village full of greenary, he enjoyed his childhood in nature, trees and plants were his friends and he got fresh air and water...he had a land and he cultivated crops in that which was fertile...then he married and lead a peaceful life, he got good profit from his agriculture...he loved his village very much because it gave him everything for his life..he had a son named Jack, Jack completed his education in town and returned to his village to lookafter his parents, but village life did not suit him , he felt that he is not able to adjust with this village life , so he asked his father to come and settle in town but his father refused and there was a lot of quarrel regarding this between father and son, finally Jack said that if they come or not he will go and settle in town and he left his old parents and went away,Jack started a business in town and earned huge profit once again he returned to his father and said come with me I have built a good house in town we will live a good life ,but father refused again, he was not ready to leave his village, then again Jack went away, as days passed jack got a new business partner Jim, Jim was very cunning he wanted to earn more money so he asked Jack to start a companies in villages as they could save some money from which was wasted for rent and other things , this seemed very good for Jack , He thought anyhow my father is not coming to town let me only go and start a factory there in the land which they have, As per the plan Jack and Jim went to his father and said that he wants to help his village people by establishing a factory and give them jobs and to develop the village, so he need his part in the land , father refused at the beginning because that land was a fertile land where so much crops were grown but due to force of Jack he gave the land to his son thinking that somehow only a piece of land he will use and that will also help his villagers , Jack and Jim was very happy they started construction and soon built one factory and started the operations very soon the factory gave a huge profit and many others also Started to build the bulidings in their lands , roads came up... vehicle's movements became more soon the village lost its all green glory , but people were very happy as they were earning more money, Joy was very sad at the changes that had happened in his village and he felt that he was a reason for that and with the grief he passed away...soon all green lands turned into buildings, rivers turned barren, all stopped agricultural activities and started businesses, as days passed there was increase in profit, and also increase in sickness most of the money was spent on helath care but no one identified the reason for the changes, suddenly there was lack of food products, water was sold in plastic bottles, soon birds and animals vanished, suddenly people started thinking why they are facing all this problem and it was because of pollution, now to breathe good air they wanted to go to vacation, for food they had to search organic shops, Jack was well settled in that place he was the richest man there , soon he also got married and he was very happy about his life, he had two children's, his childrens grew up and found a old photographs of their grandfather and village, they asked the father to take them to that place in photograph as it seemed too good , so father took them to a garden and showed them all the plants and trees, one day the younger son of Jack had a terrible disease, he took him to hospital and was ready to spend how much ever money but doctor's said the reson for this disease was pollution and unhealthy life style, how much ever he spent he could not save his son, then after few days Jim was bedridden and admitted in hospital he was in ventilator with oxygen supply after the treatment he saw the bill , it was 2000rs for one oxygen cylinder and total bill was some 3- 4 lakhs for oxygen alone, Jim started crying thinking about how precious is oxygen and the nature gives us free oxygen but for greediness we cut tress, then he understood about the importance of tress and villages but it was too late. so even we should understand how important is the nature for us and try to preserve this nature, if we take it as granted then we have to face so many problems, so let us plant tress and save this nature for future.

How can we nurture the nature that nurtures us?

* Reduce, reuse, and recycle. Cut down on what you throw away. Follow the three "R's" to conserve natural resources and landfill space.

* Vehicle pollution is one of the most significant sources of pollution. If the journey is short, walking or cycling can help reduce a lot of pollution. And, it is also beneficial to our physical wellness!

* The plantation is always the best step to start with. We should develop a habit of planting at least two small plants every weekend to support nature.

* Understanding the difference between biodegradable and non-biodegradable waste is an important step. We can learn about the same and separate the garbage in our homes based on the two categories.

* Spread the word—Be contagious! Talk to your family and friends about the actions you're taking to conserve nature. You can inspire them to make better choices for the planet we share.

STOP
Start

Save Animals
Don't cut Trees
Grow Plants
Save Water
Save Energy
Reuse
Recycle
3R
Reduce
Stop Pollution
Don't Litter

CHAPTER TWO

WHERE THERE IS A WILL THERE IS A WAY..

Everyone knows this saying in English that "Where there is a will there is a way", and this is so meaningful and it works in our daily life, it is sure that if there is a will there is surely a way, I have experienced a lot in my life....I'll share the very first experience...

It was during my school days , I joined to a new school in 8th grade and everything and everyone was new to me , I was knowing only English and Kannada languages to speak and write but most of my friends were tamilian's and many were making fun of me as I could not understand what they talk, as days passed there was a Tamil Debate Competition held in our school and without my knowledge my classmates had given my name as a participant and they wanted to make fun of me when I would not able to talk, I went to the incharge teacher and requested to cancel my name but she said it's not possible, then I was very much worried about what to do, when I informed my mom regarding this she motivated me and said this quote If there is a will there is a way, then I thought I don't even know the language what can I speak, then my mom asked my neighbour to help me, there was a sister who knew Tamil , she translated my English thoughts in Tamil and written it in English lyric, I also practiced it with full of concentration and somehow was able to manage, but on the day of competition I was literally feared because that was the first time I am facing a crowd and moreover I am talking in the language which I don't know, I had severe fever and headache but also I wanted to show my classmates what I am, so I participated and spoke in the debate, after the debate I was thinking that I should go home early, regarding prize I don't even had any idea,they started to announce the prizes like 4th prize , 3rd prize ....and when they said 2nd prize it was my name I didn't even believe I was in shock, and that saying if there is a will there is a way became reality in my life...after that I became so famous that everybody identified me as a winner , one who wanted to make fun of me was ashamed by this, later on it was a turning point in my life , I started practicipating in all competitions and I was selected for national level debate competition Speak for India. So if there is a will for surely there is a way.

CHAPTER THREE

Transformation begins with Teacher

"The Transformation of Education begins with Teacher. Teachers play a very important role in everyone's life from the beginning of education, and they become reason for

some transformation in students Life, let me share a story of how a teacher can transform a student life or education...The pillars of education is the teacher who believes in the students, loves them and moulds them...
There lived a teacher in a village who was admired by everyone, he used to teach the students lessons, values etc ..most of the students loved him very much, The teacher also loved his students more than his kids.

Once this teacher meets a boy who was begging in the streets, the teachers asks him about his education and why he is begging, the boy says that he is an orphan and he don't have anyone to take care of him, so the teacher brings him to his house and makes him to get good education and as time passed the boy will continue his education and leaves the teacher and go away, there was another student who was having no confidence, he used to always think that he cannot study once this teacher motivated him to study and as time passed he became a first class student...there were so many students whom this teacher meets in his life time and most of them were influenced by his personality, he made them understand thier potential and he helped them to identify the hidden talents and make them progress in that...as time passed most of his students became successful persons in the society, the teacher grew old and retired from teaching,the sendoff for this teacher was organised by the entire people of village all gathered there with the sense of gratitude towards the teacher who changed many students Life, one after another spoke about how the teacher influenced them, one student shared her experience about how she overcame the fear and how she was able to achieve success in her life, she shared her experience telling that once when she had almost failed in her life and decided to end her life because of the issues she was facing,she met the teacher and spoke to him , after talking to him she got courage to live and she decided to turn her failure into success, she said today i am a lawyer and all this is because of this teacher, everyone there wondered how a single person can influence so many students Life, most of his students used to come meet him and express thier gratitude.The village people also used to come and solve thier problems.

one day this teacher went to meet the District Collector regarding some issues in village, as he went in he saw a young man sitting in the chair as soon as he saw the teacher he stood up came near to him and fell on his feet, the teacher was shocked and asked who was he, the Collector said that he was the boy who was once begging and he said because of you(teacher)today i am in this position, this teacher transformed the life of a beggar to an officer, immediately the Collector sanctioned whatever help the teacher wanted to ask for the village, the teacher was very happy about his student.

This teacher transformed so many students Life, most of his students had a sense of gratitude towards him, today even we are successful because of the teachers behind us... students today need to understand the importance of getting a Good teacher, how much ever technology improves no technology can replace a teacher, students always needs a teacher, because **behind every successful person there is a great teacher who sacrificed thier life for students,** there are still some great teachers living among us to whom we should be thankful, It is possible for teachers alone to transform the person and not anyone else,that is why Kabir says in his Verse if Teacher and God both appears in front of me whose feet shall I touch, I'll touch the feet of teacher because he made me know who is God, That is the Greatness of Teachers.

The relationship between a student and a teacher is not only when they are studying with us , it is the eternal relationship as I believe that "**once a teacher is always a teacher**". I wish that there comes a day when my students grow up to be a successful people in society.

CHAPTER FOUR

Money Matters....

Money the very essential need of today's society, Money which was once a mere medium of exchange is now a very important thing in everyone's life, this is the time where many says that money matter's a lot in our day to day life, ofcourse it's very essential thing I agree but how much money do we really need is actually important, let me tell you the story..

Once there lived a old man who was nearly 80yrs , he was invited by the king of his kingdom for dinner and old man was very happy that he got an opportunity to meet the king and speak to him personally when king asked how is your life, the old man said I am very happy that I worked hard when I was young and built a house, all my children's are settled and everything is fine but I have one sorrow that before I die I should die as a rich man so I need your help to become rich , king was shocked by this and said to the old man that if I give you money all will tell that you became rich by kings money or begging from king but if you earn it you will have respect so better I'll give you a task if you complete that I will give you the reward, the old man was very happy and asked the king what was the task , king said tomorrow before sunrise come near the river which is the near palace I will tell what to do, next day old man with full of enthusiasm went near the river and king also was there then the king said to the old man that you should swim the river from that end to this each time when you complete one round you will get a gold coin worth 100gms, old man was very happy he said swimming was very easy to him and started swimming he completed one round and got a Gold coin, he was very happy and he completed another round like wise seeing the reward which he was getting old man was swimming continuously nearly he completed 50 Rounds , then king said I think you have got so much better take this and go , but old man said your majesty still sun did not set I came here during sunrise and I will go after sunset though the king advised to stop he did not stop he was very happy about being rich and wanted more money so finally he was so tired that he couldn't complete his final round that he drowned and died, the Greediness of money took away his life.As we see here he had enough money with him but he was not satisfied.

Money is something which makes people feel great today there are so many people who are rich having money but poor in humanity, and same place there are people who are poor without money but having rich heart, There is a saying that **Money is the root of all evil**, that is so true because when we see so many youngsters who have more money spend it on useless things and ruin their life, so we have to be satisfied with what we have , when we have more money we should help others in this way we can lead a peaceful life , There are so many people who try to save money in one way and lose it in other, most of the money is now spent on health, I know a person who was very rich he had money and that money made him to feel he is superior than everyone so he used to treat others without any respect one day a poor lady who was working in his house met with accident and was admitted in hospital when her children's came and asked for help that person said them that he don't have anymoney and when her children's went to hold his leg he kicked them with his leg and sent them out and somehow there was another person who helped that women and saved her, but very soon after not even a week that rich person got stroke and he couldn't even walk properly, he was not able to do anything on his own they spent lakhs of rupees but he could not become like before, he thought he had money he can buy anything but he forgot that there are things which money could not buy, Benjamin Franklin said and I quote **"Money has never made man happy, nor will it. There is nothing in its nature to produce happiness. The more of it one has, the more one wants."**

There are things in life that, no matter how much money you have, you cannot buy, but only through time and dedication will you be able to attain them let's see what are that...

- **Money cannot buy TIME.**
- **Money cannot buy HEALTH.**
- **Money cannot buy CHARACTER.**
- **Money cannot buy KN0WLEDGE.**
- **Money cannot buy TRUE HAPPINESS.**

Having more money can be important , but it can't provide everything so let's understand that how much money is required because at the end of the day there must be someone who cares for us, because nowadays due to the stress of earning money so many people will not spend time with thier families and few are always money minded that they lose the people because of that and few will change as they earn more money, some don't even bother about anything and they lose everything except money, there are many who are rich but unhappy, Money can buy all materialistic things, money can cover our basic needs and wants and provide short-term fulfillment and happiness, but if you are looking for long-term enjoyment and satisfaction, something else can give you that. **A successful life doesn't always equate to having a healthy bank account. Sometimes, the simple things around us and what's in our minds can make us feel happy and fulfilled in life.**

Money can never buy one neccesity of the soul, so lets us earn money for our need and not for greed.

CHAPTER FIVE

HUMANITY MATTERS

There is a famous saying that **"it is more blessings to give than to receive"**, and it's so true, as humans we should have humanity towards poor and downtrodden...if we help others God will help us... because it is like when we help poor we are giving alms to God, let me tell you a parable from Bible, Once many people died and they all were standing near the gates of Heaven and Hell, Then God came to choose the people who can be in heaven many were thinking that they will be in heaven as they were all famous on earth, but God selected few of them who didn't even thought they will be in heaven, so one among them asked God why did you choose me , then God said you fed me when I was hungry, You clothed me when I was naked , you gave me shelter when I was homeless and that is why I choose you to be in heaven, that man asked but when did I do it to you, God said what you did for poor is that you did for me. yes it's so true that when we help someone God will bless us, let me share with you another personal experience of me ..One evening I was standing near my home and having my tea , suddenly I saw that there was two blind people who was begging, they went near the shops and houses any very few were helping them, then I thought I have money for some other reason so it's ok if I don't help them and they passed me and went further but I was disturbed a lot in my heart so I went near them and gave them the money I had , I was relieved but evening I wanted to pay the money for some needs, but I thought God will look over it, I just went and sat in my home someone who had to give money from long time sent me the money which was triple the times what I helped them, so I have such so many experiences where God gave me more than what I gave, so it is very important that we will learn to help others , sometimes we waste so much money in unwanted things but we feel very difficult to help people, today 10rs is not a matter for many but there are people who needs that 10rs for their food, so instead of wasting money on junk food and other bad habits if you give that to the needy, you will be blessed, let's learn to give from what we have, we think only rich people should can give, but the truth is if you are rich at heart you can also help...I tell rupee per day if you save also 30rs for month and that 30rs can feed someone, it's just an example it's up to you that how you can help others.

How can we help others...

* Poverty has no RELIGION- For helping a poor person you should have broad mind of thinking. First of all you should know that poverty has no religion.Religion teaches you to have compassion for people around you. All religions are the same and GOD is one.

* Collect your old clothes and donate- If you get bored from your clothes and wanted to get rid of them. Don't throw them away in fact collect them and give them to those who has need them.Not only this, try to encourage your friends and colleagues to join you and to do some charity.

* After party and function give remaining food to needy- It happens most of the time that after a party or function so much food remained.Do not throw it. Give that food to hungry and needy people. This is better to fill someone stomach than to dump it in garbage.

* Talk into your youth group- Not only the parents even the youth can be helpful in your charity. The youths are the saplings for society.If they become helpful to the downtrodden and the poor than society will also become prosperous. Make groups, organize charity events and spread the word 'Help the poor and needy'.

* Buy books for poor child who can't afford- As we have said education gives light and direction to one's life. So, always try to help the poor at least in education.If you see a child around you who cannot afford books for studies then try to buy that child books. You can also give your previous classes books to that child if you have not studying them. Don't sell back to the book shop.

*Donate a part of your earning to the poor and needy- If you see a person around you is so poor that cannot meet to her/his basic needs. You can do one thing in this case.You can daily save little money from that allowance and after sometime that little money can be proved helpful to the poor.

If we have two let's give one to others , **let's teach the future generations that it's blessings to give than to receive.**

CHAPTER SIX

THE TRUE VALENTINE

There lived a boy and two girls, the boy's name was Valentine and the Girls name was Rosy and Ruby, They all were classmates studying together from thier childhood, Valentine was a Good boy with warm personality and eager to learn things, Rosy was an intelligent and responsible girl, but Ruby was always a mischievous and problematic girl...Thier childhood passed with all the good memories, but as they reached thier teen age the real problem started, since they were childhood friends they used to discuss everything and do things , as days passed Valentine was influenced by Rosy and Ruby but in different ways, Rosy always wanted him to concentrate on his studies and achieve his Goals and see him as a successful person but Ruby wanted him to enjoy the teenage like all others , It was very difficult for him to take a decision on whose friendship he should continue whether Ruby or Rosy, there was a reason for his confusion because whatever Rosy said to him seemed like old fashioned and difficult,but whatever Ruby said was like it was correct example, Whenever they wanted to go out Rosy insisted him to inform to parents and return early, but Ruby used to tell him that it's not so important to inform parents everything whatever they do, when Valentine won a scholarship, Rosy said him to save it for his further education but Ruby said to spend it on a vacation, By all this experience now Valentine wanted to decide that whose friendship is helpful to him, whether it is Rosy or Ruby..

By the time of this confusion they completed their high school ,Valentine and Rosy passed with Very Good percentage, but Ruby somehow managed to get pass marks, now they have entered thier college, here there was a break for the friendship of Rosy and Valentine, because Rosy had to go abroad for further studies, by this even the confusion of valentine was cleared that he will continue his friendship with Ruby, As days passed Ruby was not giving any importance for studies and she always dreamt that Teenage is for enjoyment, the same thing she made Valentine to believe, and even he started listening to her and forgot about his studies and his parents struggle behind educating him, the case was similar in Ruby's life also, her parents were also working hard to meet her needs but she never bothered about that....as time passed she was influenced by social media and made many friends, even motivated Valentine to use that...she totally involved in Virtual world losing her values and dignity for likes and comments, Valentine was also misleaded by Ruby both of them didn't even care about thier studies nor about their hardworking parents, there was lots of backlogs as each year passed, Valentine who was dominated by Ruby thought she would be a right life partner for him, Ruby had a different idea she was interested in enjoying life than valuing life....When Valentine said about his plan about marrying her she also agreed, As there were lots of backlogs, he didn't complete his education, his parents who lost hope in him were worried about his future but for him now life was Ruby not anything else, so he started working as a Daily wager, all his earnings would go for the expenses of Ruby's needs (Selfish needs), he could not understand that, and he never bothered or payed anything for his parents who had so much Dream about their son, ...things were going like this one fine day Ruby met another boy who was well settled, she soon started avoiding Valentine and finally said to him that she was not interested in marrying a person who does work for daily wages and rejected him, Valentine was heartbroken he couldn't understand what to do.....he had so much dreams about his life with Ruby , now he realised the value of his parents whom he neglected for the sake of Ruby, and also remembered Rosy who wanted to see him as a successful person....he was depressed about his life ....it took him long Time to recover from the pain , but he was helpless because all the opportunity he had earlier was not there now, neither he could go back to college nor he could get any good job, by this time Rosy returned from abroad completing her studies, she was excited to see what her friends are doing because there was no any contact between them for all those years she went abroad, she thought valentine would have been settled in some Good company in higher position, but when she met him she was shocked seeing him in that condition, even Valentine was ashamed about his life , then Rosy spoke to him and made him realise how important it is to decide with whom are we influenced, she said that she was thinking that he was her dream life partner but never said to him because she thought they should not get distracted while studying, she had a great plans for their life not about present but about future but valentine gave importance for enjoying present life than future and ended up with depression.

So it it always important for us to understand who is important, who is influencing us and how are we influenced whether Good or Bad , the Valentine as his name could not understand who is his true Valentine (Love) because of the teenage enthusiasm about life he choose to enjoy his life when he wanted to study and now leading a life of unhappy, So better be careful about when to do what because **We reap what we sow.**

CHAPTER SEVEN

BEFORE IT'S TOO LATE....

Life gives us more opportunities to succeed in life, but most of us sometimes will not understand that due to the negligency or sometimes wantedly we will miss so many opportunities and later regret thinking that I must have done it earlier, I listen to so many people who says I had a good opportunity to settle in life but due to my habits or negligency I couldn't do that and they tell my kids should not do the same mistake so I am working hard, most of the children's also regret later for not listening to their parents or teachers.

Once there was a boy named Tom, he was a very good boy was listening to his parents and teachers, he was also a topper in the school but as he went into High school his behaviour started changing he did not listen to his parents neither teachers, he indulged in so many mischievous acts did not concentrate properly during his 10th standard, teachers tried to advise him but he did not listen finally he failed in all the subjects, he was not least bothered about it, as days passed he joined with bad friends and spoiled his life, finally after 5 years he came to meet his teacher and started to cry, he said now he is understanding the importance of education and he wanted to write the exams now, but as per the rule he missed all 5 re-attempts chances and now was unable to write exams , but the teacher helped him to write exam as a private candidate and he passed the exam, but he could not get good job he started working in so many places as they were removing him very soon from all the places , he was totally depressed about his life. Through this what we can understand is that he had all the opportunity to study well but due to his negligence he spoiled his life and by the time he realised it was too late. I can tell you my another experience which happened in recent days I went to my home town during holidays, there I boarded into an auto and was going to my home from the bus station, The auto driver was wearing mask and even I was also wearing mask so we couldn't identify each other, Auto driver stopped auto to fill the fuel during that time I met a person who was well known to me he greeted me and spoke very respectfully, listening to our conversation the auto driver asked about myself then I started telling about all myself and he asked me about where did I study then I said him about my school, class which year and everything then he also said he too studied in same school, class and also in same year and when we removed our mask we identified each other that we were classmates, then we spoke about our school days and remembered all our teachers, during our conversation he said it's so true what our teachers said that if you study well then you can settle in life with good job otherwise you have to work hard later, so he felt sad about himself telling that now he is realising the value of time and education, he said when I used to see you at school I used to feel that you are not enjoying your teenage that you were always into academics and culturals, there was times when I and my friends used to laugh at the way you was , but today you are in good position whereas we are suffering now by saying this he was very emotional.

So it is very important for us to understand the opportunities that the life will give us, if we misunderstand the life then we will end up with sorrow, let's do what's right in right time though it's difficult because "**Difficult roads always leads to beautiful destinations**". Before it's too late realise your mistakes and rejuvenate yourself.

9 798889 516163

Printed by Libri Plureos GmbH in Hamburg, Germany